THE ENCHANTED COOKIE TREE

PAVILION
CHILDREN'S

This edition first published in 2010 by
Pavilion Children's Books
10 Southcombe Street
London W14 0RA
An imprint of Anova Books Company Ltd

Text copyright © Helen Nathan 2010
Illustrations © Catherine Black 2010
Design layout © Kevin Shaw 2010
Cover design © Anova Books 2010
Photographs © Anova Books 2010

10 9 8 7 6 5 4 3 2 1

ISBN 9781843651604

Printed by 1010 Printing International Ltd, China

This book can be ordered direct from the publisher at the website: www.anovabooks.com

Dedications:
To Carol (and her next door neighbours!) with love and thanks. (HN)

For Peter, thank you for choosing the roller coaster ride and your unwavering support and positivity. (CB)

Acknowledgments:
To Mary Young and Premier food for believing in Flossie and her magic. To Araminta Whitley at L.A.W. and Polly Powell and her team at Anova who came to my rescue at the eleventh hour. Nicole, I think you're great, Kevin, feel the love, and of course to Larry who is completely wonderful and Molly, Rosie and Lottie who make life brilliant. Finally thanks to Carolyn and her team at cakes4fun for recreating all my cakes and biscuits and making them look so beautiful.

Be sure to wash your hands before baking or cooking and always ask a grown up to put things in and take things out of the oven. McDougalls flour is highly recommended for all your baking needs. It makes cakes rise like magic!

Please visit Flossie's web site, where you can find more baking hints and recipes, join her fan club and go to the online shop where you can purchase special baking items and ingredients. You can see how to make the crown cookie on the front cover at the website too! Every time you see a * next to an ingredient, this means you can buy from:

www.flossiecrums.com

Do you know what happens when you've got fairies living at the bottom of your garden? Well, one minute you're drawing quietly in your bedroom at 22 Maple Syrup Lane and the next you're off to Romolonia on another fairytale adventure...

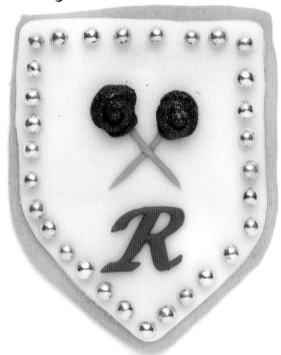

A note for fairy fans

See if you can find a fairy on every page – sometimes you might have to look really hard to find them. Grown ups will often miss them, so you might have to help.

I was lying on my bed quietly drawing when my brother Billie started yelling: "FLOSSIE! Flossie, come and look at this!"

I jumped so much that my pink crayon shot across the page, ruining my picture of a strawberry frosted cupcake.

"Stop yelling Billie," I said crossly. I waved my picture in front of his nose. "Look what you made me do."

"But Flossie," whispered Billie. "There's something funny happening in the garden!" Billie was staring out at the garden through his binoculars. "There's a little tree moving all by itself!"

"What?" Don't be so silly!" I grabbed the binoculars out of Billie's hands and looked out at the wet, dripping garden.

"Near the chestnut tree," whispered Billie. And then I saw what Billie was talking about. The little tree was shaking and standing next to it were two tiny figures.

"It's Plum and Crystal!" I gasped. "What are they doing?"

Dropping the binoculars on the bed, I grabbed Billie's hand. "Come on," I said. "The fairies are back!"

We thundered downstairs, pulled on our wellies and raced out into the garden.

Poor Plum and Crystal. They were standing in the soggy flower bed looking very sorry for themselves. Their beautiful wings were wet and drooping and Crystal's tiny blue slippers were covered in mud.

"Hello Flossie. Hello Billie," said Plum sadly. "We're trying to dig up this tree, but it's so difficult with just this little spade."

"I'll help you," said Billie kindly. "I'll get my big spade from the shed."

Billie raced off across the garden and was back in a flash with his spade. In two minutes the little tree was out of the ground.

"You should be called 'Billie the Strong'!" said Crystal, giving Billie a shy smile. "We've been struggling for hours."

Billie blushed and looked very pleased with himself.

"But why were you digging up the tree?" I asked.

"For the Royal Welcoming, of course," said Plum.

A Royal Welcoming! I jumped up and down and clapped my hands. This was the best news ever! A Royal Welcoming meant there was a new royal baby in Romolonia.

But Plum was looking crossly at Crystal. "You weren't supposed to tell Flossie," she said. "Cherry was going to tell Flossie."

"Oh Flossie, please don't tell anyone I told you," begged Crystal. "It just slipped out."

"Don't worry," I said. "I won't say a word."

"Come on Crystal," said Plum, looking at her watch. "We've got to go now. Bye Flossie, bye Billie... Thanks for helping us."

Billie and I watched as the two fairies flew round and round the little tree.

They flew faster and faster, leaving a trail of tiny stars behind them. The tree grew smaller and smaller until it was tiny enough for the fairies to carry it away.

As I lay in bed that evening, I was sure that I'd never be able to get to sleep after all the excitement. But I must have drifted off because just before dawn, I was woken up by the sound of voices arguing.

"Let's throw water on her, that'll wake her up."

"No Minty, that's mean – just whisper in her ear."

"I tried that already, Cherry, but she's as deaf as a dormouse. I'm just going to wiggle her nose a bit."

It felt as if a fly had landed on my nose so I swatted it away – accidentally pushing Minty halfway up my left nostril.

"Oh yuck! That was disgusting," said Minty. "Check my head Cherry, I think I've got bogies in my hair."

By now I was fully awake. "Minty! Cherry! You're really here."

I sat up in bed, blinking and yawning while the little fairies flitted in front of me.

"Sorry to wake you Flossie," Cherry said gently. "But we've got the most exciting news..."

"Queen Rosie and King Saffron have had a baby!" Minty cried. She was so excited, she leapt into the air and accidentally banged her head on a shelf. "A beautiful baby girl called Princess Cauliflower!"

"Not Cauliflower!" Cherry laughed. "*Corn*flower!"

"Oh yes, Cornflower, that's right. She is sooooo beautiful, Flossie. She's got curly blonde hands and tiny hair... I mean curly blonde hair and tiny hands and the bluest eyes you have ever seen. They're as blue as... ummmm, let me think... as blue as... what are they as blue as Cherry?"

"Cornflowers?" suggested Cherry.

"Yes, cornflowers! And there's going to be a Royal Welcoming in the Ice Palace."

"A fairy princess baby," I said dreamily. "How I would love to see her."

"Of course you'll see her", said Minty. "Queen Rosie wants you to make the iced cookies for the Welcoming Tree, silly!"

"You see Flossie," said Cherry. "It's our tradition that when a baby is welcomed, everyone hangs cookies on the Welcoming Tree. Then Queen Rosie takes her Crystal Star Wand and..."

"Stop!" cried Minty. "Don't spoil the surprise. Flossie will see for herself." Outside my bedroom window the sky was turning pink and the birds were starting to sing.

"Jumping jelly beans!" said Minty. "It's late, we have to go. See you in Romolonia, Flossie."

"Sweet dreams," said Cherry. In the blink of an eye, the fairies were gone. Sweet dreams?! There was no time for sleeping now! There were cookies to design, with sweets and sparkling glitter! I grabbed my sketchpad and pens and started to draw.

As soon as I finished, I raced in to see Mum, Dad and Billie to tell them everything that had happened.

"Iced cookies!" said Billie. "I love iced cookies. Can I make them too?"

"You can," Mum replied. "But I think you've both forgotten that today is Saturday and that means clean sheets and tidying your room!"

"But my room is tidy!" cried Billie. This was a huge fib – Billie's room is always a disaster zone.

I was almost finished cleaning my room, when I heard Mum yelling "BILLIE CRUMS! What is all this?"

So I went to see what was happening.

Mum was kneeling on the carpet holding up Billie's duvet. A week's worth of toys and clothes were crammed under his bed. We left Billie to sort out his room and Mum and I went downstairs, put our aprons on and got to work.

Royal Welcoming Cookies
(makes about 20 cookies)

What you need:

280g plain flour

2 egg yolks

200g unsalted butter

100g icing sugar

1 tsp vanilla essence

Cookie cutters (you can use a dress, unicorn or pram cutter* like we have here, or choose your own shapes!)

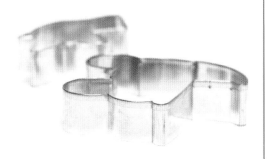

What you do:
Step 1 – Making the dough

Grease a 35 x 25cm baking tray.

Rub the butter and flour together, using just your fingertips, until the mixture looks like breadcrumbs.

Add the sugar, vanilla essence and egg yolks to the mixing bowl and stir well until the mixture forms a ball.

Pop the ball into the fridge for half an hour.

You can also make the dough with a food processor – but ask a grown up to help you!

Step 2 – Rolling out the dough

Ask a grown up to turn the oven on to 200°C.

Sprinkle a handful of flour on the table and rub a bit of flour on your rolling pin. Start rolling out the dough, but every so often, wiggle the dough around to check that it's not sticking to the table. If it is, start again with a bit more flour.

When it's rolled out the dough should be about as thick as a pound coin.

Get your cutters and start stamping out your cookies!

Use a blunt knife to lift them really carefully onto the baking tray. You can place the cookies close together because they won't spread.

Take a toothpick and make a hole through the top of the cookies so that you can thread a piece of string through to hang them once they're iced.

Ask a grown up to put them in the oven and bake the cookies for 8 minutes, then take them out and leave them to cool.

While Mum was putting on her oven gloves I carefully picked up the heavy mixing bowl and swung around to put it in the sink, but as I turned I got a big fright.

Two scruffy little creatures with beady eyes and pointed noses were staring in through the window, their eyes fixed on the cookies. They pointed to the window catch, wanting me to open it and let them in.

"Go away!" I yelled through the closed window. "These cookies aren't for you."

"Who are you talking to?" asked Mum.

"The two imps at the window," I said. "They want me to let them in."

"Well don't," said Mum turning to look. "They look like they just want to take our cookies."

"Don't worry, I won't," I said. "Shoo, shoo." One of the imps stuck his tongue out at me and then they both disappeared.

It was when Mum was putting the first batch of cookies into the oven that I saw something which really made me jump.

A horrible, big black spider was hanging up in the corner of the kitchen.

"MMMMUUUUUMMMM!!!!!!!!!!!!!!!!!!!!!!!!!!!!!!!!!!!!"

"Goodness Flossie," said Mum. "You nearly made me drop the cookies! What is it?"

"There's a big, ugly, hairy spider up there!"

"Oh for heaven's sake Flossie – that's not a big spider and besides, it's not hurting anybody."

"It has to go," I cried. "I can't bake cookies with that in the room. It might jump on me!"

"Well I am a bit hairy," said the spider in a rather posh voice. "But I think the word 'ugly' is quite harsh. And why would I want to jump on you?"

Now, I know I chat to fairies in my bedroom, but a talking spider in the kitchen? That's just bonkers!

"Allow me to introduce myself," he said. "My name is Geoffrey, and I was sent here by Queen Rosie and King Saffron. When you work for the Royal Family, you have to have spider security."

"Well, I'm very pleased to meet you Geoffrey," said Mum kindly. "We welcome you to our home, don't we Flossie?"

"I suppose so," I said, though I was still worried. But then I had a brilliant idea. "You know who you should meet Geoffrey? My brother, Billie – he loves bugs and creepy crawlies."

"Really?" said Geoffrey. "And where would I find this delightful person?"

"He's upstairs in his bedroom. Perhaps you could help him tidy it up!"

I watched Geoffrey scuttle away and shuddered. At least he wasn't in the kitchen anymore and I could concentrate on the cookies.

As soon the cookies were ready to come out of the oven, Mum told me to go upstairs and check on Billie.

As I hopped up the stairs I heard the spookiest noise coming from Billie's room, like the sound of rushing wind. I stopped outside and listened. Then from behind the door I heard a voice...

Laws of goodness,
Spells of right,
Magic means and magic might,
Banish darkness, bring on light,
Help put this upset room right!

There was a sudden flash of light from under the door which made me jump. I threw open the door just in time to see a toy truck disappear into Billie's toy box all by itself!

I gasped. "Billie, what is going on?"

"Nothing," said Billie, shrugging his shoulders. "I was just cleaning my room and Geoffrey was helping me."

There was no time to ask what was *really* going on, we had a lot of cookies to ice!

Icing the Cookies

Unicorn

What you need:

White ready-to-roll icing

Black writing icing

Edible silver glitter*

Edible glue*

What you do:

1. Roll out white ready-to-roll icing and cut out unicorn shape.
2. Glue the icing shape carefully onto the cookie.
3. Use black writing icing to draw unicorn's eye, cover horn with silver glitter and use tiny strips of white ready-to-roll icing to make the mane.

Welcoming Robe

What you need:

Pale blue and white ready-to-roll icing

Textured rolling pin*

Mini flower cutter*

Edible glue*

Mini edible pearls

What you do:

1. Roll out blue icing and roll over with the textured 'flower' rolling pin.
2. Cut out welcoming robe and place carefully onto cookie using edible glue.
3. Lift the bottom edge of the robe using a skewer to make the folds – make sure you ask an adult to help you with this.
4. Use mini flower cutter to make flowers and decorate with flowers and ribbon made from white ready-to-roll icing.

Baby's Pram

What you need:

White and pink ready-to-roll icing

Pink ribbon

Icing nozzle*

Quilting tool*

What you do:

1. Roll out white ready-to-roll icing and cut out pram shape. Carefully stick onto cookie.
2. Cut out small pink icing circles for wheels (using circular cutter or bottle top) and make the spokes by squishing the top of an icing nozzle into the centre of the wheel.
3. Use the quilting tool to score lines on the pram.
4. Decorate with pink ribbon and pink writing icing.

Romolonian Shield

What you need:

Ready-to-roll white and red icing

Silver balls

Red edible glitter*

Mini rose 3-D mould*

Alphabet 'Tappits'*

What you do:

1. Roll out the white icing, and cut out the shield.

2. Glue onto cookie with edible glue. Push the silver balls around the edge.

3. Make two small balls of red icing (about the size of your thumb nail) and push into the 3-D moulds. Tap them out and hey presto! Two sweet little roses to cover with glitter.

4. Make the stems with green icing writing.

5. Tap out a letter 'R' from the alphabet 'Tappit' and glue onto shield.

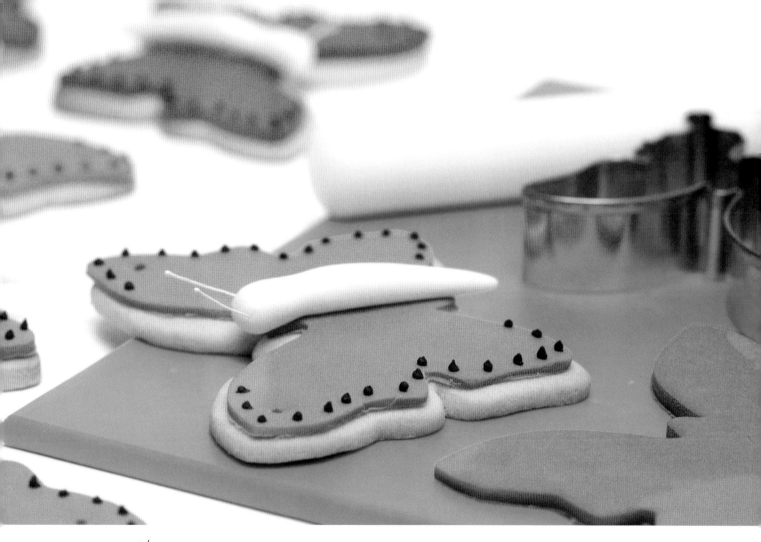

Butterfly Cookies

What you need:

Ready-to-roll icing in your favourite
colours

White-ready-to roll icing

Chocolate flavoured writing icing

Flower stamens*

Pearly shimmer*

What you do:

1. Roll out the coloured icing and stamp out the butterfly shapes.
2. Stick carefully onto the cookies.
3. Dot chocolate dots with the writing icing around the edge of the butterfly wings.
4. Make the body by rolling a small ball of white icing between your palms.
5. Poke the stamens into the butterfly to make the antennae.
6. Sprinkle shimmer dust on the body and then place onto the cookie.

We were just putting the final touches of glitter to the cookies when there was a soft tapping at the window. I jumped, thinking it was those pesky imps again but it was Candy, the head fairy.

Mum opened the window latch and Candy fluttered inside, her glossy brown curls bouncing and shining in the kitchen light. She looked very pretty, but a bit cross.

"Everyone's waiting for you!" she exclaimed, but then she saw the cookies. "Oh, they're so beautiful! Queen Rosie will be so happy. But please, we must hurry. It's very bad manners to keep the Royal Family waiting."

"We've just finished," I said, pulling off my apron and brushing icing sugar off my sleeves.

We picked up our tray and hurried across the garden to the big chestnut tree where a tiny door magically appeared.

Candy flew around us. Around and around she went, tiny stars trailing behind her, as we became smaller and smaller.

"I'm scared Flossie," said Billie. "What if I don't get big again? Then I won't be Billie the Strong anymore."

"You will get big again," I replied. "I promise!" Billie still looked worried.

But then the door to Romolonia swung open and Billie was so surprised, he forgot to be scared anymore.

I had forgotten how beautiful Romolonia was. Glowing lanterns lit our way as we followed the fairies along a corridor of trees filled with shining golden apples.

"Come along, come along," said Candy, sternly. "Stop goggling like goldfish. We mustn't keep the King and Queen waiting."

Billie and I walked as quickly as we could without dropping the cookies.

Then we turned a corner and in front of us were two enormous doors, which looked as if they were made of frosted glass. The doors magically opened for us and we entered the most beautiful room I had ever seen.

"Hurry up, hurry up," cried Candy. "Haven't you two ever seen an Ice Palace before?"

Inside, all the fairies and elves were lined up on either side of a silver carpet and everyone clapped and cheered as we walked in with our trays. At the end of the carpet holding the new baby was Queen Rosie and standing next to her was King Saffron. They both wore beautiful white and silver outfits and silver crowns on their heads. Crystal wands sparkled at their waists. Behind them was the little tree from our garden, but it wasn't little any more – it was enormous!

I felt very nervous. King Saffron looked like a happy jolly man but Queen Rosie can be grumpy at times. As we got closer, the Queen smiled and bent down to show us Princess Cornflower, who was sleeping (and even more beautiful than I had imagined!)

Queen Rosie nodded to the fairies and one by one they came forward to choose a cookie from the trays. Then they each flew up to the Welcoming Tree and hung their cookie on one of the tree's branches.

When all the cookies were on the tree, a small fairy appeared holding a white cushion. In the middle of the cushion rested a silver heart.

"That's the magic silver heart," whispered Cherry, who had flown to my side. "See what happens next."

The giant tree began to shake. I thought it must be the beginning of the magic, but it wasn't…

"IMPS!" yelled King Saffron. "Those imps are trying to steal the cookies!"

"SECURITY SPIDERS!" he thundered. "ARREST THOSE IMPS!"

About a hundred spiders dropped down from the ceiling onto the tree. They tried to catch the imps but I don't think they were having much luck because some of the fairies jumped in to help. The tree began to shake rather a lot and then it started to sway and then it started to fall…

…right in the direction of the Royal Family!

Everyone gasped, but we were all too shocked to move.

And that's when Billie sprang into action!

He grabbed the crystal wand from Queen Rosie, held it up in the air and closed his eyes.

"Laws-of-goodness-spells-of-right-magic-means-and-magic-might-banish-darkness-bring-on-light-and-put-this-upset-tree... RIGHT!"

The tree stopped in midair and then slowly returned to being upright again. For a few seconds there was complete silence.

And then everyone began to cheer and pat Billie on the back.

Two of the fairies lifted him into the air and Billie's face beamed with happiness.

And those two naughty imps were finally caught and taken away by our very own Geoffrey and another security spider.

When everyone had settled down and stopped cheering and patting Billie's back, Queen Rosie beckoned Billie forward.

"I have heard about your strength," she said in a gentle voice. "But you are not only strong, you are brave too. From now on you will be known as Sir Billie the Brave."

Awarded for Bravery

She waved her wand and a solid gold medal on a red ribbon appeared around Billie's neck. Billie looked like he would burst with pride!

It was time to continue the ceremony. Queen Rosie picked up the silver heart again. Up she flew to the Welcoming Tree and placed the silver heart at the very top. The tree began to shudder and shake... Oh no, I thought, not imps again! But it wasn't... One by one the branches started to sparkle and glimmer until the whole tree was shimmering as though it was covered in diamonds. Just as we thought it couldn't be any more beautiful, silver fireworks exploded above our heads, lighting up the Ice Palace in a silvery shower.

Queen Rosie gently took Princess Cornflower from King Saffron's arms and lifted her high in the air.

Billie and I gasped as we watched the royal baby sprout two tiny wings. The Queen kissed the princess on both cheeks and the baby laughed and shrieked with delight.

"Use your magic well, my child," said Queen Rosie.

Sweet little Honey was suddenly at my side. "Did you guess what was going to happen?"

"No," I said, "I never would have guessed in a million years!"

Billie looked at his medal for the hundredth time. "I wish we could stay here," he said. "I won't be Sir Billie the Brave when we get back home."

"Yes you will," I said. "You'll be Sir Billie the Brave wherever you go. You'll have your medal to prove it."

It was time for Minty and Cherry to take us home again.

Mum was dying to hear about everything that had happened. You should have seen her face when Billie showed her his medal.

Later that evening when Mum was reading us a story, I started wondering how long it would be before I saw my fairy friends again and I felt quite sad.

"I bet we never have an adventure like that again," I said.

"Oh I don't know about that," said Mum. "Another adventure is always just around the corner."

The End...

... I have to go now but I can't say goodbye without sharing a few more recipes with you from our adventures in Romolonia. I wonder if you can spot where I got the ideas from!

Don't forget to wash your hands and put your apron on, then turn the page and start baking!

Geoffrey's Marshmallow Chocolate Cookies (makes about 20 cookies)

If I'm going to eat spiders, they have to be made of chocolate!

(If you don't want to cook the chocolate biscuit base, you could cheat and buy biscuits, just have fun with the decorations, however the chocolate biscuit recipe is delicious!)

What you need:

230g plain flour
50g cocoa powder
200g butter
2 egg yolks
100g icing sugar

Decorations:

Chocolate marshmallow tea cakes
(for the body)
red strawberry laces (for the legs)
ready to roll white icing
black writing icing (for the eyes)
edible glue* (or 2 tbsp icing sugar
mixed with 2 tsp water)

What you do:

1. Ask a grown up to turn the oven on to 200°C.

2. Mix together the flour, cocoa and butter until they resemble breadcrumbs. Add the sugar and egg yolks to the mixing bowl and stir well. Leave the mixture to cool in the fridge for half an hour.

You can also make the dough with a food processor – but ask a grown up to help you!

3. Stamp out round cookies. I use the top of a jar of mum's coffee.

4. Bake the biscuits for 8 minutes then ask a grown up to take them out the oven.

5. When the cookie has cooled, add Geoffrey's body and legs using the edible glue. Glue a marshmallow teacake onto the cookie, then poke the red laces into the body and glue them in (you'll have to use a coocktail stick to poke them in.)

6. Stick in some googly eyes by rolling little balls of white ready to roll icing and dot with black writing icing, then 'glue' onto Geoffrey's body.

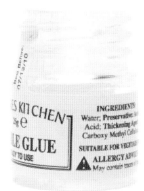

Glittering Ice Palace Cookies with Coconut and White Chocolate
(makes 12 cookies)

(If you hate coconut like Billie does, just leave it out.)

What you need:

150g self raising flour

2 tbsp condensed milk

115g caster sugar

75g white chocolate, broken into chunks

115g softened butter

50g desiccated coconut

Decorations:

2 tbsp caster sugar

White edible glitter*

What you do:

1. Ask a grown up to turn the oven on to 180°C.
2. Beat the butter and sugar together until it is all mixed together.
3. Stir in the condensed milk.
4. Add the flour, white chocolate and coconut and then work the mixture into a soft dough (You'll have to use your hands, so make sure they're clean!)
5. Break off small pieces of dough (about the size of a ping-pong ball) and place on a greased baking tray then squish the cookie just a little. You'll get about 6 cookies on a tray.
6. Bake for 12–15 minutes, or until edges are slightly golden.
7. Ask a grown up to take them out and leave to cool.
8. Dust with caster sugar, then edible white glitter.

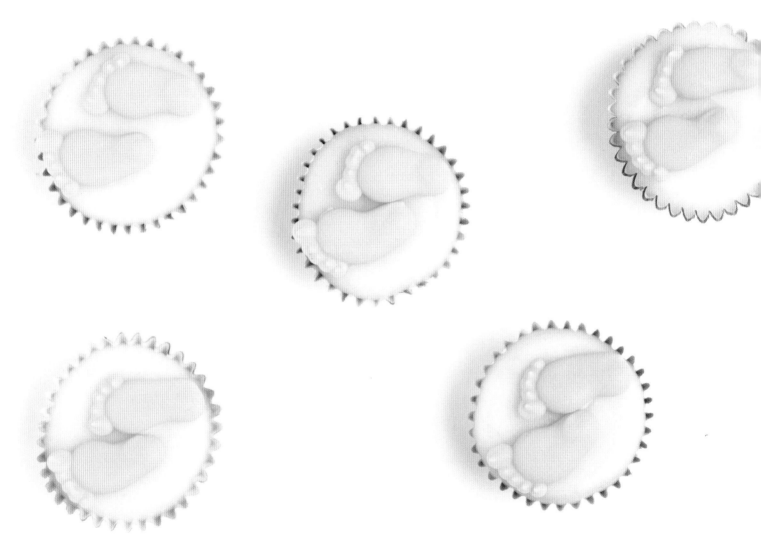

Mini Footprint Baby Cakes
(makes 24 cakes)

What you need:

55g self-raising flour

1 dessertspoon milk

55g caster sugar

1 egg, beaten

55g softened butter

Packet of mini cake cases
(sometimes used to make
homemade chocolates)

Icing and Decorations:

200g icing sugar

2 tbsp fresh lemon juice

1 tsp water

One packet of baby footprints*
(or you could use pink or pale
blue sweets)

What you do:

1. Ask a grown up to turn the oven on to 190°C.
2. Mix all the mini cake ingredients together in a bowl.
3. When they're well mixed, place 24 mini cases onto a baking sheet and spoon 1 teaspoon of mixture into each case.
4. Bake for 15 min then ask a grown up to take them out.
5. Cool the cakes.
6. Mix the icing sugar, lemon and water together to make a smooth paste, then spread half a teaspoon of icing on each cake.
7. Place two tiny feet on each cake.

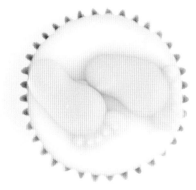

22 Maple Syrup Lane Cupcakes with maple icing

(makes 12 cupcakes)

What you need:

115g self-raising flour

115g softened butter

100g caster sugar

2 eggs, beaten

1 tbsp milk

Icing:

400g icing sugar

50g melted butter

4 tbsp maple syrup

1 tsp cold water

Decorations:

Edible flowers or
bugs and numbers*
Re-usable picket fence cupcake
wrappers* (or you can design
your own.)

What you do:

1. Ask a grown up to turn on the oven to 190°C.
2. Mix all the cupcake ingredients together in a bowl.
3. When the ingredients are well mixed, place twelve cupcake cases in a twelve-hole cupcake tin and spoon in the mixture.
4. Bake for 18 minutes then ask a grown up to take them out.
5. Leave to cool.
6. Make the icing by mixing all the ingredients together.
7. Spread on the icing (or pipe it on if you have a piping bag)
8. Decorate!

Princess Cornflower's Pink Meringue Kisses with rose cream

(makes 48 meringues = 24 kisses)

What you need:

125g caster sugar

2 egg whites

1 small drop of pink
food colouring

200ml double cream

2 drops of rose water (available
from most supermarkets)

Decorations:

Edible white glitter*

What you do:

1. Ask a grown up to turn the oven on to 140°C.
2. Whisk egg whites with an electric mixer for about 3 minutes or until they are quite stiff.
3. Keep whisking while you add the sugar, one dessertspoon at a time (I count to twenty between each spoonful) until your meringue looks like little shiny mountains, then mix in the pink food colouring.
4. Lay greaseproof paper on two baking trays and smear with butter. (Or use 2 silicone mats if you have them)
5. Place teaspoon-sized blobs of meringue onto your trays (I used a piping bag so they look just like little kisses!) and bake in the oven for 1½ hours.
6. Ask a grown up to take them out of the oven and leave to cool.
7. Whisk the double cream with two drops of the rosewater, then sandwich two meringues together to make a delicious 'kiss'.
8. Sprinkle with edible glitter.

Here are a few helpful baking tips that I wanted to share with you...

1. Wash your hands when you are baking – fairies don't like germs.
2. Mum says it's healthier to cook with natural ingredients because they're better for you.
3. It's a good idea to wear an apron so you don't get too mucky. (Can't see the point myself but Mum wanted me to write that down.)
4. Always ask a grown-up to put things in and take things out of the oven for you.
5. Licking the spoon and bowl is yummy, but it is dangerous if you have used raw eggs. If you smile sweetly, you might be allowed to lick the icing bowl after you have finished decorating your fairy cakes.
6. If you enjoy cooking, always help to tidy up. My mum gets really cross if I just run off and play before everything is clean and tidy. (Washing up can be quite fun really.)

www.flossiecrums.com

Conversions

Dry Measurements

METRIC	IMPERIAL
15g	$^1/_2$oz
30g	1oz
60g	2oz
90g	3oz
125g	4oz ($^1/_4$lb)
155g	5oz
185g	6oz
220g	7oz
250g	8oz ($^1/_2$lb)

Liquid Measurements

METRIC	IMPERIAL	US CUPS
30ml	1fl oz	$^1/_8$ cup
60ml	2fl oz	$^1/_4$ cup
90ml	3fl oz	$^3/_8$ cup
120ml	4fl oz	$^1/_2$ cup
140ml	5fl oz	$^2/_3$ cup
170ml	6fl oz	$^3/_4$ cup
200ml	7fl oz	$^7/_8$ cup
230ml	8fl oz	1 cup
260ml	9fl oz	$1^1/_8$ cups
290ml	10fl oz	$1^1/_4$ cups
500ml	17½fl oz	2 cups